Murdoch Mole's
Big Idea

Georgie Adams
Illustrated by Chris Fisher

Orion
Children's Books

Murdoch Mole's Big Idea was originally published
in 1995 by Orion Children's Books
This edition first published in Great Britain in 2013
by Orion Children's Books
a division of the Orion Publishing Group Ltd
Orion House
5 Upper Saint Martin's Lane
London WC2H 9EA
An Hachette UK Company

3 5 7 9 10 8 6 4 2

A catalogue record for this book
is available from the British Library.

ISBN 978 1 4440 0824 1

Printed and bound in China

www.orionbooks.co.uk

For Tom and the moles
on Trebursye Hill

The oak tree, which had stood for over two hundred years, blew down on Monday morning.

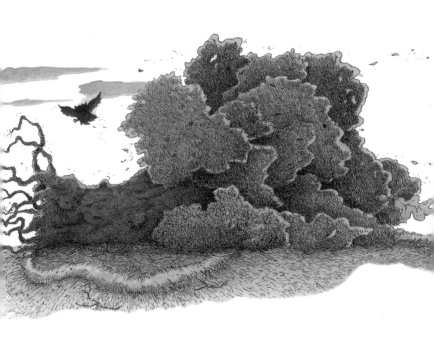

Bert watched the tree fall.
"I'm impressed," he said.
"Did I do that?" said
Murdoch Mole.

"I saw it with my own eyes,"
said Bert. "One minute you were
tunnelling. Next thing, whoosh!
The tree fell down."

"Wow!" said Murdoch.

On Tuesday Murdoch was in
the vegetable garden looking for
worms. He was peeping under
a cabbage leaf when he thought
he saw one. It was the biggest
worm he had ever seen.

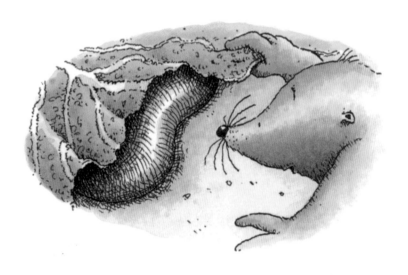

But when Murdoch grabbed
it for lunch, a jet of water shot
into the air.

"Brilliant!
A bird-bath," said Bert.

"Did I do that?"
said Murdoch.

"There it is," replied Bert,
"and full of birds already!"

14

On Wednesday Murdoch dug a new tunnel. It went around the oak tree …

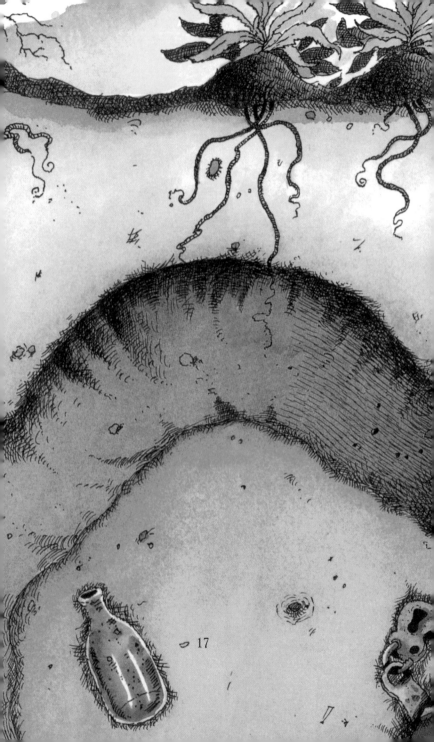

17

... past the vegetable patch ...

… and under the wall.

Murdoch was wondering where he was when the earth shook.

That was followed by a very loud whirring noise.

Murdoch clawed his way up.
It took him longer than usual,
but at last he reached the top.

"Amazing!" said Bert. "The
biggest molehill in the world."

"Did I do that?" said Murdoch, looking down from a great height.

"All by yourself," said Bert
with a grin.

Murdoch jumped up and down
excitedly.

At home that evening,
Murdoch sat in his favourite
chair.

He thought about the tree,
and the bird-bath. He thought
about the molehill – the biggest
molehill in the world!

And that gave Murdoch
an idea.

A big idea.

Murdoch's idea was to turn his molehill into a tourist attraction.

It would be famous!

Visit the biggest molehill in the World! Spectacular views guided tours by Murdoch Mole.

On Thursday morning
Murdoch found some chalk and
a piece of wood and made a sign.

Then he set off.

He thought there would
probably be some early visitors
to his molehill and Murdoch
was keen to show them around.

There was no one waiting for him.

In fact, Murdoch couldn't see anything at all.

He looked carefully to make
sure he was in the right place.
He was. But the biggest molehill
in the world had disappeared.

Murdoch thought of his big idea.

There was no time to lose.

He would have to start again.

Murdoch worked hard all day.
From time to time he popped
his head above the ground to
have a look, but his molehill
was no bigger than, well …
a molehill.

Owl, who had been watching,
flew down.

"What *are* you doing?"
she asked.

"Making the biggest molehill in the world," replied Murdoch. "*Another* one."

And he told Owl what had happened.

"Oh dear!" said Owl. "A
bulldozer did all that, not you.
It was clearing the ground for a
new road. It wasn't a molehill.
Just a big pile of earth."

Murdoch looked very sad.

"Bert said I made it," he said,
"and I believed him."

"It was Bert's idea of fun,"
said Owl crossly.

38

Murdoch felt useless.
A nobody. A very ordinary
mole with silly big ideas.

As they were talking, Duck
came along.

"There is something you could
do," said Duck. "Something you
do very well."

"What's that?" said Murdoch
gloomily.

"Dig a tunnel," said Duck.

"Why do you need a tunnel, Duck?" said Murdoch.

"I don't," said Duck. "But I know someone who does."

Duck waddled off and came back with … Toad!

Toad looked upset.

"I can't get home," she said. "My pond is on the other side of the new road."

"Which is where the tunnel comes in," explained Duck.

"Leave this to me," said Murdoch.

Murdoch disappeared
underground while Owl, Duck,
Toad and some friends waited
on top.

Murdoch dug all through
Friday and Saturday.

By Sunday the job was done.

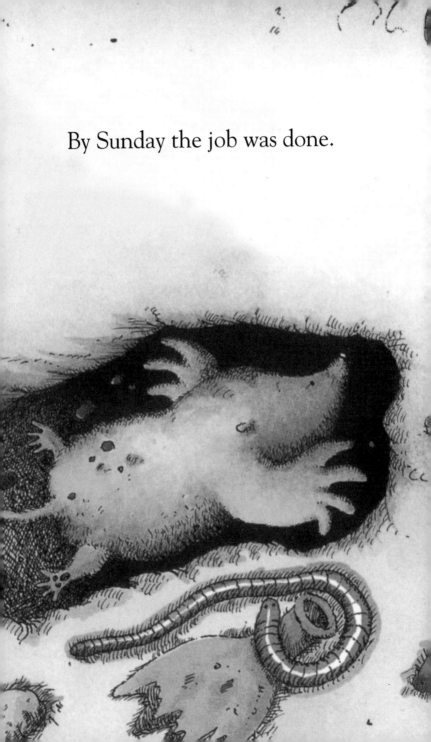

Murdoch's Tunnel (as it was called) went right under the new road.

Thanks to Murdoch, Toad and other small animals could cross safely from one side to the other.

Everyone cheered. Murdoch was tired, but happy.

He felt he had done something Really Useful.

He was wanted after all. He was a *somebody*.

Bert came to see what all the fuss was about.

"Did you do that?" said Bert.

"All by myself!" said Murdoch proudly.

"You're very clever!" said Bert.

"Thank you," said Murdoch.

And because something deep down inside told him that Bert really meant it this time …
Murdoch believed him!

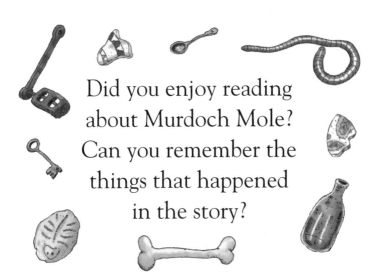

Did you enjoy reading
about Murdoch Mole?
Can you remember the
things that happened
in the story?

What happened to the oak tree
on Monday morning?

What did Murdoch Mole find
on Tuesday?

What happened when Murdoch
grabbed the worm?

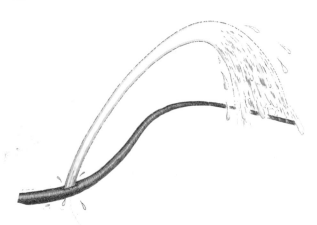

Where did Murdoch sit to think?

What was Murdoch's first big idea?

What did Duck tell Murdoch he could do?

Who was upset because she couldn't get home?

Who told Murdoch he was
a genius?

What are you going to read next?

More adventures with

or go to sea with

Horrid Henry,

Poppy the Pirate Dog,

or into space with

Cudweed.

You could have fun on

A Rainbow Shopping Day,

or explore

Down in the Jungle,

but watch out for

A Creepy Crawly Story!

Make magic with

The Three Little Witches,

and have
a ball
with

Princesses.

Or follow the star in

The First Christmas.

Enjoy all the Early Readers.

the
orion star

Sign up for newsletter
for all the latest children's book news,
plus activity sheets, exclusive competitions,
author interviews, pre-publication extracts
and more.

www.orionbooks.co.uk/newsletters

Follow @the_orionstar on .

Orion
Children's Books